The
Little
Golden
Lamb

retold by Ellin Greene

illustrated by Rosanne Litzinger

Clarion Books • New York

Clarion Books
a Houghton Mifflin Company imprint
215 Park Avenue South, New York, NY 10003
Text copyright © 2000 by Ellin Greene
Illustrations copyright © 2000 by Rosanne Litzinger

Type for this book was set in 16-point Cantoria MT.
Illustrations were executed in fine watercolors and colored pencil.
Book design by Janet Pedersen.

This retelling is based on a version of "The Lamb with the Golden Fleece"
that originally appeared in *Magyar Folk-Tales* (Folk-lore Society, 1886).

Printed in the USA.

Library of Congress Cataloging-in-Publication Data

Greene, Ellin, 1927–
The little golden lamb / retold by Ellin Greene ; illustrated by Rosanne Litzinger.
p. cm.
Summary: A retelling of the traditional tale in which a poor but goodhearted lad finds his
fortune with the aid of a little golden lamb to which everyone who touches it sticks.
ISBN 0-395-71526-1
[1. Folklore.] I. Litzinger, Rosanne, ill. II. Title.
PZ8.1.G785L1   2000
398.22—dc21
[E]   99-36025
CIP

WOZ 10 9 8 7 6 5 4 3 2 1

For Mom and the Florida gals,
with special thanks to Madeline
—E.G.

A toast to Dinah Stevenson, whose wit, forbearance,
and gentle persuasion kept me on course
—R.L.

There once lived a poor man whose wife died, leaving their little son motherless. The man cared for his son as best he could, but as soon as the lad was old enough to be on his own, he sent him out into the wide world to seek his fortune.

The lad set out with only the clothes on his back, a small parcel of food, and a flute that his father had made to cheer him on his journey. He walked and walked, practicing his flute along the way to keep up his spirits.

At last he came to a sheep farm and the farmer hired him to look after the sheep. All day long the lad drove the sheep from place to place, always looking for the sweetest grass and clover, and playing a merry tune on his flute. The farmer was so pleased with the lad's work that he promised him whatever wages the lad asked for at the end of a year.

In the spring a lamb was born with a golden fleece. When it was barely able to stand, the shepherd lad began to play his flute and the lamb began to dance. It looked so comical kicking up its heels and wagging its tail that the shepherd lad shook with laughter. From then on, whenever the shepherd lad played his flute, the little golden lamb would frolic to the music.

The shepherd lad became very fond of the lamb and decided not to ask the farmer for any wages, but only for the little golden lamb. The farmer was fond of the lamb himself, but a promise is a promise, so at the end of the year he gave the little golden lamb to the shepherd lad. He added a gold coin and wished the lad well.

The lad set off for home with the little golden lamb. On the way he stopped at an inn for supper and a night's lodging. At the inn he heard that the king's daughter was suffering from a strange illness, but if she could be made to laugh, she would be cured at once. The king was offering three bags of gold to anyone who could make the princess laugh.

The shepherd lad ate his supper and, tired from his journey, went to bed early and soon fell fast asleep. In his sleep he dreamed of the princess and the three bags of gold.

While he was sleeping, the innkeeper's daughter came into his room to pet the little golden lamb. She had in mind to steal it, you know, but just then her hand stuck fast to the lamb's tail. She could not get it loose, no matter how hard she tried. When the lad woke up, he couldn't free her hand either, so there was nothing for it but to take the girl with him.

As they walked down the road, the shepherd lad began to play his flute. The little golden lamb kicked up its heels and began to dance, and the girl on the lamb's tail danced too.

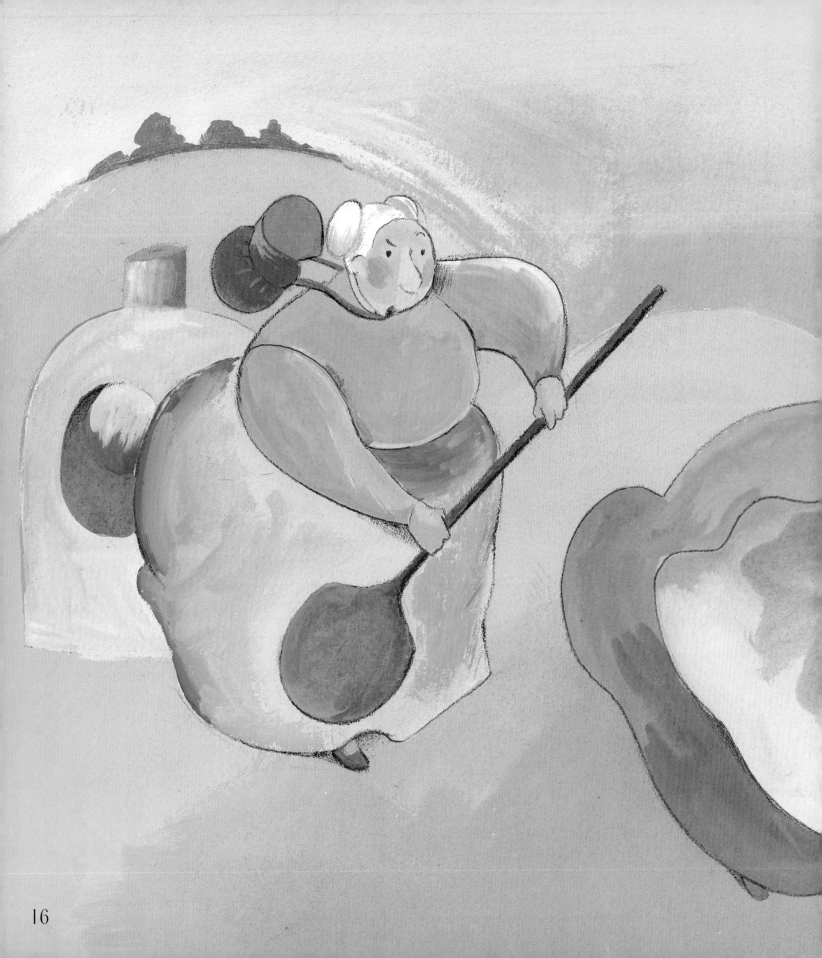

They passed an old woman who was putting bread in the oven to bake. "Don't make such a fool of yourself!" the old woman snapped when she saw the girl holding on to the lamb's tail and dancing. When the girl continued to dance, the old woman gave her a whack with her baker's peel. The moment the peel touched the girl, it stuck fast, and the old woman stuck to the peel, and the little golden lamb carried them all, dancing down the road.

The merry procession continued on its way. As they passed a church, a priest came out and saw the strange sight. "Stop this foolishness," he scolded. When the old woman and the girl continued to dance, the priest tapped the old woman's shoulder with his cane. But the moment the cane touched the old woman, it stuck fast, and the priest stuck to the end of the cane.

19

Down the road they went,
The shepherd lad playing his flute,
The little golden lamb kicking up its heels,
On the lamb's tail the girl,
On the girl's back the baker's peel,
On the baker's peel the old woman,
On the old woman the cane,
On the cane the priest,
And the little golden lamb carried them all,
dancing down the road.

Toward evening they came to the king's castle, and it happened that just at that moment the princess was leaning out her window. When she saw the little golden lamb dancing, followed by the merry procession, she burst out laughing. At the sound, the king rushed to see what had made the princess laugh.

And when the king saw the little golden lamb dancing, and on the lamb's tail the girl, on the girl's back the baker's peel, on the baker's peel the old woman, on the old woman the cane, on the cane the priest, and the little golden lamb carrying them all, dancing down the road, the king laughed so hard he couldn't stop.

This made the little golden lamb so glad that it shook everything and everyone off its back, and the lamb,

the girl,

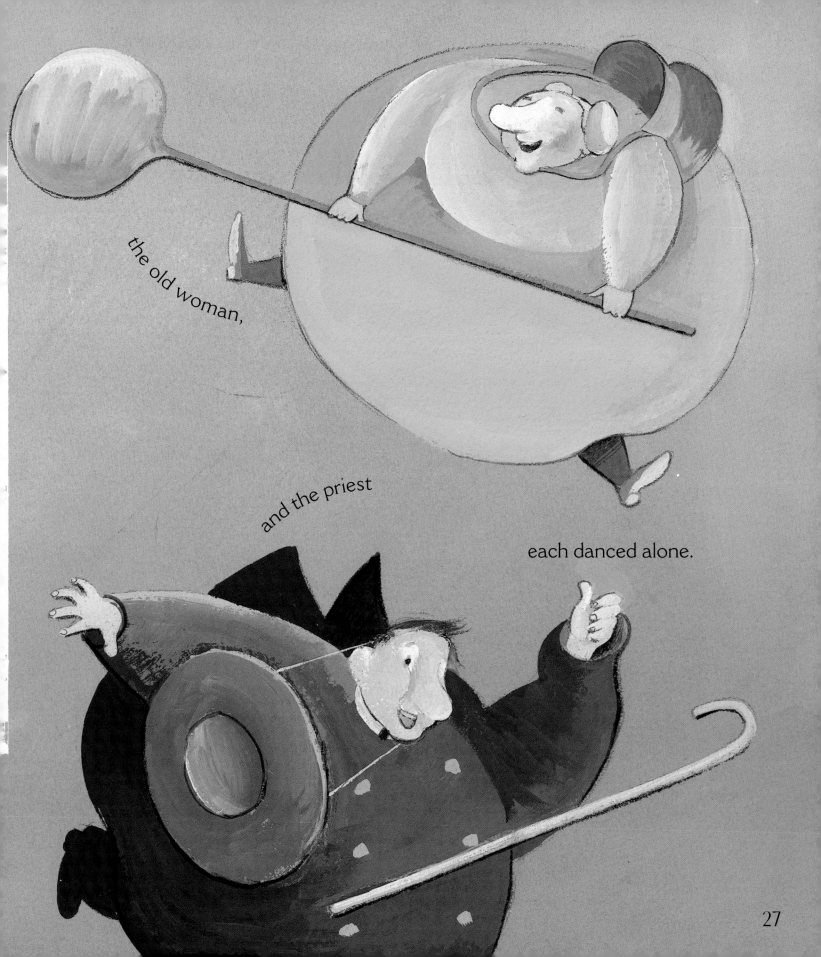

the old woman,

and the priest

each danced alone.

27

The king gave the shepherd lad the three bags of gold as promised and invited him to come and live in the castle. The shepherd lad sent for his father so that he might share his son's good fortune.

In time, the shepherd lad and the princess were married. The priest performed the ceremony, the old woman baked the wedding cake, the innkeeper's daughter served the cake at the wedding banquet, and the little golden lamb, who had grown into a big golden ram, sat in a place of honor at the head table.

The shepherd lad and the princess lived
with merry hearts all the days of their lives.

And so may we.